The Job

by Susan Hartley • illustrated by Anita DuFalla

"I have a job," said Dan.

"I can put jam on it."

"I can put jam on it for Jen.
I can put jam on it for Jim."

"Come and get it!" said Dan.
"Come have jam with me."

"In a jiff," said Jen.
"I want to see the jet."
"The man is in the jet,"
said Jim.

Tim can come and get it.

No jam for Jen and Jim,
but Dan and Tim can have
the jam!